BOOM

BOOM

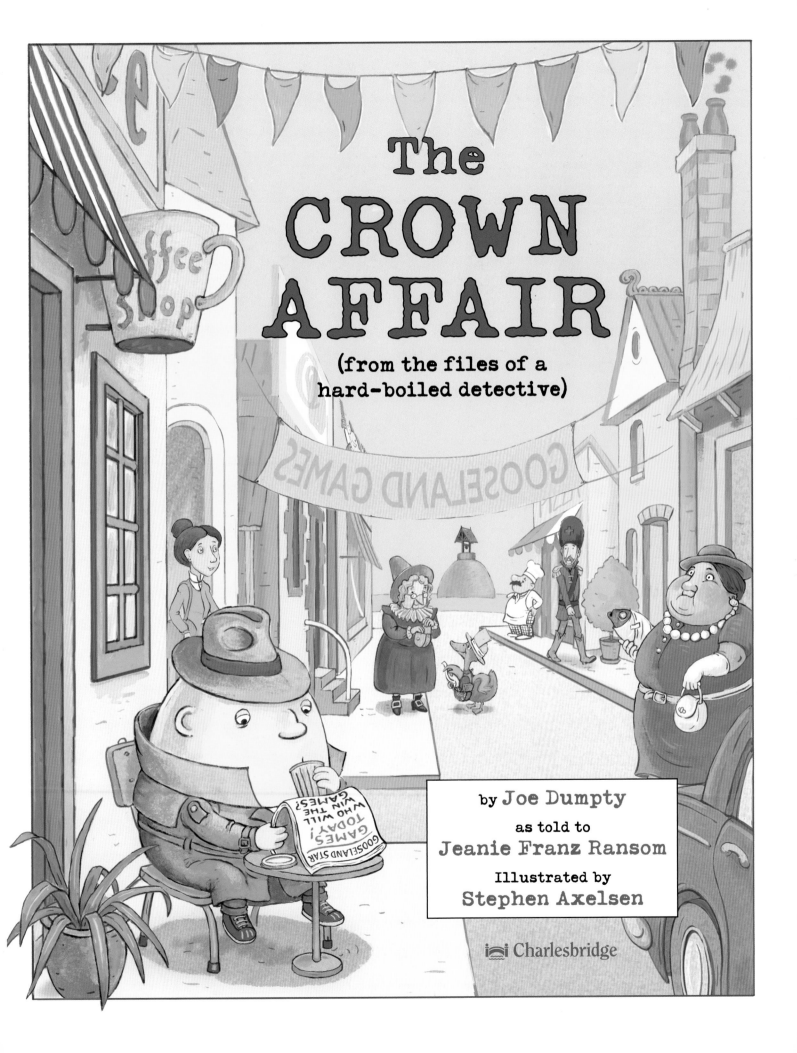

The CROWN AFFAIR

(from the files of a hard-boiled detective)

by Joe Dumpty

as told to Jeanie Franz Ransom

Illustrated by Stephen Axelsen

Charlesbridge

To my eggcellent family and all the good eggs in my critique group
—J. F. R.

For my dearest daughter, Lauren Rose
—S. A.

Published by Charlesbridge
85 Main Street
Watertown, MA 02472
(617) 926-0329
www.charlesbridge.com

Library of Congress Cataloging-in-Publication Data
Ransom, Jeanie Franz, 1957–
   The Crown Affair / Jeanie Franz Ransom; illustrated by Stephen Axelsen.
      p. cm.
   Summary: Just before the Mother Gooseland Games, hard-boiled detective Joe
Dumpty is called upon to solve the mystery of what made Jack and Jill fall
down the hill—and who took Jack's prized crown after the fall.
   ISBN 978-1-58089-552-1 (reinforced for library use)
   ISBN 978-1-60734-757-6 (ebook)
   ISBN 978-1-60734-642-5 (ebook pdf)
1. Nursery rhymes—Juvenile fiction. 2. Detective and mystery stories.
3. Humorous stories. [1. Characters in literature—Fiction. 2. Mystery and
detective stories. 3. Humorous stories.] I. Axelsen, Stephen, illustrator. II. Title.
PZ7.R1744Cr 2014
[E]—dc23   2013049019

Printed in China
(hc) 10 9 8 7 6 5 4 3 2 1

Illustrations done in Photoshop on a Wacom Cintiq 22hd and a Wacom Intuos
Display type set in Typeka by T-26
Text type set in American Typewriter by International Typeface Corporation
   and Blambot Pro by Nate Piekos
Color separations by KHL Chroma Graphics, Singapore
C & C Offset Printing Co. Ltd. in Shenzhen, Guangdong, China
Production supervision by Brian G. Walker
Designed by Diane M. Earley

Jack and Jill went up the hill
to fetch a pail of water.
Jack fell down and lost his crown . . .

And that's where I come in.
Who am I? I'm Joe Dumpty, Private Investigator.

I'm the go-to guy for detective work in Mother Gooseland. I cracked the Humpty Dumpty case when I figured out that my brother Humpty didn't just *accidentally* fall from that wall. Chief Goose still can't wrap her beak around the fact that I've solved more crimes than her gaggle of police geese. So it must have ruffled her feathers when Jill gave me a jingle.

"Jack's crown is missing," Jill said. "Chief Goose thinks he just *lost* it. But I'm sure someone took it! If that crown isn't found by two o'clock today, the Gooseland Games will be canceled!" Jill sighed. "I told Jack not to wear that crown except on special occasions. Will you take the case, Joe?"

I'm one tough egg, but I've got a soft shell for damsels in distress. Not to mention, I'm the biggest Gooseland Games fan this side of Old Mother Hubbard's house.

"Consider it taken," I said.

When I rolled up to the Hill, All the King's Horses and
All the King's Men were loading Jack onto a stretcher.

"Joe, I'm so glad you're here," Jill said.

"How's Jack?" I asked. "Can I talk to him?"

"Suit yourself," Chief Goose interrupted. "I'll check
on my team. They're bound to turn up that crown soon."

I went over to talk to Jack. "Hey," I said. "It's Joe Dumpty."

Jack's eyes flew open. He looked right at me. "It's Jack," he said.

"No," I said. "It's Joe. Joe Dumpty, Private Investigator."

"It's Jack! Jack! Jack, I tell you!" Jack shouted.

Was this a clue?

Jill shook her head. "That fall must've scrambled his brains!"

How I hate that word *scrambled*. But I'm hard-boiled enough not to show any reaction. I pulled out my notebook.

"Let's take it from the top, Jill."

"Jack and I went up the Hill," Jill said. "But all of a sudden, there was this big *BOOM*, *BOOM*, *BOOM* overhead. The ground shook, and Jack and I both fell down."

"When did you notice the crown was missing?" I asked.

"Not right away," Jill replied. "First, I checked on Jack. Then I called 9-1-1. After that, it's a blur. I was a little dizzy myself. I came tumbling down after, you know?"

Fall or no fall, Jill's always been a little dizzy.

"Jill," I said, "I need you to focus. Did you see anyone either before or after your fall?"

"I thought I saw someone run by after we fell," Jill answered. "But it's hard to say who. Maybe it was someone getting ready for the race today."

Maybe. But why would they steal the crown when they had a chance to win it fair and square this afternoon?

Looks like this case won't be over easy.

"I'm going to lay an egg if I can't get to the Games by two to honk the starting horn," Chief Goose interrupted.

Everyone was going to lay a whole dozen eggs if the crown wasn't found and the Games had to be canceled.

Thankfully, Spider arrived. Ever since the Humpty Dumpty case, Spider's been doing legwork for me. He's got sharp eyes, too. If he couldn't spot a crown hiding in all this grass, nobody could.

Spider got busy combing the area.

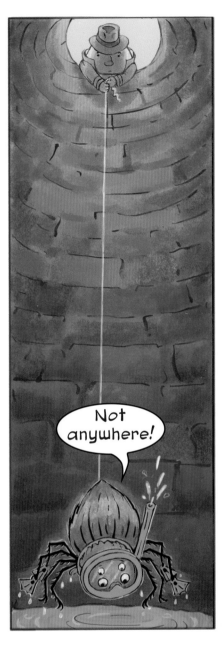

But just as I suspected, the crown was long gone. Someone had to have taken it. I whipped out my notebook and reviewed what clues I had so far.

Wow. Not much. Just Jack repeating the name "Jack." Do you know how many Jacks live in Mother Gooseland? I decided to start with the closest one.

As I approached Jack Sprat's place, I heard two people fighting.

Could they be fighting about the crown? My yolk trembled as I knocked on the door.

It swung open, and there were the Sprats, playing tug-of-war with . . .

"What IS that?" I asked.

"It's a red herring," Jack Sprat said.

"I was about to fry it, but he wants it broiled,"
Mrs. Sprat added.

Jack Sprat could eat no fat. His wife could eat no
lean. Apparently it made it tough for them to agree on
how to fix their fish. But they did agree on something.

"We both felt an earthquake," Jack Sprat said when
I asked if they'd seen or heard anything that morning.

"See anyone?" I asked.

"Not until now, when you showed up,"
Mrs. Sprat said.

"You might want to talk to our
neighbor," Mr. Sprat said. "He's always
out racing around."

I thanked the Sprats and headed next door.

At first I didn't think Jack B. Nimble was home,
because normally he'd answer on the first knock.
I waited. And waited. Until . . .

. . . the door finally opened, and I saw why Jack
had taken so long to answer.

"What happened to you?" I asked.

Jack invited me in. "This morning," he said, "I was
practicing my candlestick jump, when this big *BOOM*,
BOOM, *BOOM* shook the house! I tripped, fell, and
hurt my foot."

"Sounds painful," I said.

"You don't know the half of it," Jack said. "When I landed, I ended up sitting on the candle."

You look bummed.

Between his bum foot and his scorched bottom, Jack wouldn't have been nimble—or quick—enough to grab the crown this morning.

"What do you think that *BOOM* was?" I asked.

"Maybe you should ask Jack Hammer," Jack B. Nimble said. "He's always building something."

When I knocked on the door of the House that Jack
Built, a familiar blonde answered.

"What are you doing here?" I asked.

"I'm house-sitting for Jack Hammer," Goldy said.
"He's been out of town all week."

Out of town? I was running out of suspects, unless
Goldy knew something—or someone.

"Where were you around eight this morning?"
I asked.

"Seriously? I never get up before noon," Goldy said. "But this morning, a loud *BOOM* woke me, so I went out for breakfast. The Muffin Man serves a sweet bowl of porridge."

"See anyone while you were out?" I asked.

"Yes, I literally ran into a dude I went to nursery school with," Goldy said. "Jack . . . Jack what's-his-name. He was muttering something about a crown. You might be able to catch him at the Muffin Man's."

Another Jack!
Another lead!

Sure enough, when I got to the Muffin Man's Bake Shoppe, there was Little Jack Horner, sitting in the corner.

"Word on the street is the Gooseland Games crown's gone missing," Little Jack said. "And Jill hired you to find it."

"Ah, but I heard that you needed a crown," I said accusingly.

Little Jack smiled wide and pointed. "Thanks to a cracked tooth from a plum pit, I've already got a crown—from the dentist."

There goes that lead, I thought. "Any idea who'd take the crown?"

"I don't know," Little Jack said. "But on my way here, a guy ran by me lightning fast! I thought maybe he was someone practicing for the race today."

"Did you get a good look at him?" I asked.

"I didn't," Little Jack said. "But he dropped this."

There was only one person who could have dropped this magic bean. But that person wasn't even allowed in Downtown Gooseland. Not after he'd been caught stealing from the Giant.

It was time to find Jack Beanstalk.

Jack Beanstalk's mom still lived on a farm outside of town. I'd heard she'd grounded Jack for life after he did jail time for stealing from the Giant and was banned from the Gooseland Games. Maybe Ms. Beanstalk knew where I could find her son.

I called Spider and told him where I was going—and why. Then I asked him to do something for me. "Could you take a run up the Beanstalk and look around? Maybe you can catch the Giant at home."

When Jack's mom opened the door, I showed her
the magic bean Little Jack Horner had given me.

"Where'd that come from?" she asked.

"Somewhere your son wasn't supposed to be," I said.
"He dropped it this morning in Downtown Gooseland."

"That's impossible," Jack's mom said. "Jack's been
in his room all day."

My phone rang as I followed Jack's mom into the house. It was Spider.

"I'm with the Giant," he said. "Jack tried to run off with a bag of the Giant's gold today. When the Giant told him to stop, Jack laughed and taunted the poor guy until he was hopping mad. The Giant then chased Jack, who dropped the bag of gold and disappeared down the beanstalk."

"When did this happen?" I asked.

"Around eight," Spider said.

Eight? That's when everyone felt the ground shaking. It must have been the Giant running after Jack!

Jack wasn't in his room. But the window was open.
I stuck my head out and looked around. It would be a
crime to have to cancel the Games on such a bright,
sunny day. I checked my watch. Almost two o'clock.

Almost too late.

That's when I saw a flash of gold in the trees. Thank you, Mr. Sun. Things were looking up. I called Spider back and told him to hurry over.

I pointed out the window. "Is there something over there?" I asked Jack's mom.

"Just Jack's old tree house," she said.

I raced outside and saw a ladder nailed to the side of
a tree. Where was Spider when I needed him? I looked up,
and there was Jack Beanstalk, wearing the missing crown!

"Jack Beanstalk, bring that crown down right now!"
I shouted. "It's not yours!"

"It is now," Jack said. "Finders keepers!"

Jack Beanstalk had to have been the guy Jack and Jill saw running by the Well. And he must have been the one who'd almost knocked down Little Jack Horner. Jack Hill had indeed been trying to clue me in on who'd taken the crown. But I knew there was more to the story.

"You didn't just take the crown, Beanstalk," I said.
"You made sure to taunt the Giant first, to get him to
chase you. You knew he'd shake all of Mother Gooseland,
and Jack and Jill wouldn't stand a chance of staying on
their feet. Then you slid down the Beanstalk and grabbed
the crown off the ground."

Jack Beanstalk smirked slyly. "Timing is everything."

"It'll be your fault if the Gooseland Games are canceled because you stole the crown," I said. "Do you want to ruin it for everyone?"

"I don't care," Jack said. "I can't compete in that dumb old race anyway. Besides, everyone knows I can run faster and climb higher than anyone in Mother Gooseland. The crown should be mine!"

Don't egg me on!

WAY!

WRONG

BACK!

GO

PRIVATE KEEP OUT

NO GIANTS

"It would have been yours if you hadn't tested positive for magic beans at the finish line last year," I said. "Bring that crown down right now!"

"Come and get it," Jack Beanstalk said. "Oh, wait. You can't. You Dumpty boys are scared of heights."

"But *I'm* not," Spider said, soaring onto the scene. I almost laughed. Jack Beanstalk was jumping around like he had beans in his britches. This guy could steal from a giant but was scared of an itsy-bitsy spider? The crown slipped off his head. I held out my hat, hoping that my experience as catcher for the Gooseland Gagglers would serve me well.

Eeek! A spider!

WAY

WRONG

BACK!

PRIVATE KEEP OUT

NO GIANTS

Yes!

"Keep your eyes on him," I told Spider. "I have to get this crown to Chief Goose before the Games are canceled!"

"Good work, Joe," Chief Goose said. "You came through for everyone in Mother Gooseland. And great hustle getting the crown here. Maybe next year you should run in the Games."

I smiled and shook my head.

"Thanks, Chief," I said, "but I think I'll stick to running after bad guys. . . ."

"I've just gotten word
that the Cow jumped
over the moon, and no
one's seen her since."
It's time for this egg to
get cracking again.